John Harrold.

This book belongs to:

....

Contents

Illustrated by **John Harrold**
Story colouring by **Gina Hart**
Original stories by **James Henderson**
and **Ian Robinson**
Adapted by **Sue McGeever**

RUPERT

The
EXPRESS NEWSPAPERS
Annual

John Harrold.

Published by Express Newspapers, 10 Lower Thames Street, London EC3R 6AE. A Northern & Shell Media Company.
Email: rupert.bear@express.co.uk. First published 2004.

No. 69 **£7.50**

Rupert strides out in the strong breeze - "Great! I can fly my kite with ease."

It is a bright, sunny day with a strong breeze stirring the tops of the trees. "Just right for kite flying!" cries Rupert as he sets out towards the common. "Have fun!" calls his Mummy, standing by the garden gate. "Don't be back too late!" Rupert races to the top of the hill and sees his pal, Bill Badger. "Hello, Bill!" he calls. "Come up here and help me fly my new kite!"

the Sky Pirates

He runs along - Bill Badger's there.
"Let's fly my kite up in the air."

"Please hold on tightly," warns young Bill -
As Rupert stands high on the hill.

Bill is delighted to see that Rupert has a kite and hurries up to join him. "Hold on tight!" calls Bill. "I'm going to let her go!" He throws the kite up into the air and cheers as Rupert pulls on the string. The kite soars higher and higher. As they look up they suddenly see a large, dark cloud overhead. "How strange," says Bill looking puzzled. "It's the only cloud in the whole sky!"

Then suddenly a cloud draws nigh
Up in the sparkling clear blue sky.

RUPERT
loses his kite

Now Rupert's kite cannot be seen -
So backwards on the string they lean.

All at once the string snaps in two.
The kite is gone – what will they do?

They run to tell the others how
A cloud has got their kite right now.

"That cloud just took our kite away!"
"Good joke," laughs Edward. "Now let's play."

The kite gets nearer and nearer to the dark cloud until it vanishes inside. Rupert pulls the string but, to his surprise, the kite doesn't move. The chums pull on the string with all their might but the kite still won't move! "W...what's happening?" gasps Bill. Then the string snaps and the pair tumble backwards...

Rupert and Bill scramble to their feet and gaze up in disbelief as the dark cloud drifts slowly on its way with their kite inside. "Let's go and tell the others," says Rupert, seeing his friends nearby. "Good joke!" laughs Edward Trunk, shaking his head. "But, I think your kite simply blew away..."

RUPERT

sees his ball hit a cloud

Cricket is fun the pals agree
And Rupert hits out mightily.

There is a clang. The pals all shout -
As Algy catches Rupert out!

"Well, goodness gracious!" they all cry.
"The ball was bounced back by the sky!"

Rupert's puzzled and wonders why -
There's more to this than meets the eye!

The pals decide to have a game of cricket and Rupert soon forgets all about his missing kite. Rupert is batting and gives the ball a mighty thwack sending it high up into the air. The next moment the ball hits the black cloud with a clang, plummeting back to earth to be caught by an astonished Algy...

"Gosh!" gasps Edward. "It must be the same cloud we saw earlier!" cries Bill. "There aren't any others in the sky." "Look!" says Rupert and points towards the cloud. Although it has been drifting slowly until now, it suddenly seems to pick up speed and has soon disappeared in the direction of Nutwood...

RUPERT

tells his Mummy and Daddy

Rupert decides to tell his Dad,
Of the strange morning he has had.

"The Professor may have a hunch,"
Says Dad, "go see him after lunch."

As Rupert tells the Prof. what's up
Bodkin starts packing one more cup!

They place the hamper in the boot,
Jump in the car and off they scoot.

Abandoning the game, Rupert hurries home to tell his parents about the strange cloud. "Sounds like a problem for the Old Professor! Why don't you talk to him?" laughs Rupert's Daddy. "By the way, there's a picture of him in this morning's paper. It seems he's invented some sort of machine for making gold!"

The Professor and Bodkin are getting ready to go out on a picnic. "Come and join us," urges the Professor after he has heard Rupert's story. "You can keep a watch on the sky in case the cloud comes back and enjoy a picnic tea at the same time!" They load the hamper into the car and set off...

RUPERT

sees the cloud again

"We'd better follow it and see
The reason for this mystery."

They drive into the countryside -
To have their picnic they decide.

"Oh goodness me," exclaims our bear.
"There is the cloud high in the air."

To the Prof.'s tower the cloud goes
Sinking down low so nothing shows.

Rupert asks the Professor about his new machine for making gold. "Oh dear," his friend sighs. "A complete failure, I'm afraid. I can use it to make beautiful gold coins, but after a while they all turn into worthless lead..." Suddenly Rupert gives a cry. "Over there!" he calls. "The dark cloud has come back!"

"Good gracious!" exclaims the Professor. "It's hovering over my tower!" To the Professor's astonishment the cloud sinks lower and lower until the top of the tower is completely hidden from view. "How extraordinary!" he declares. "Quickly everybody. Back into the car! We must find out what's going on!"

Returning to the tower they hurry -
Up the stairs and to the study.

Why – someone's broken in – but how?
Doors and windows are all locked now.

Bod, dashing up the turret stair
Cries: "Look! A ladder's dangling there!"

He grabs the ladder - off he sails.
"Oh, help me please!" poor Bodkin wails.

When they arrive at the Professor's tower the dark cloud is still there. They hurry upstairs to his study but as the door opens Rupert sees that the floor is covered in a jumble of scattered papers. "Somebody's broken in!" he cries. "Yes," gasps the Professor. "But how? Everything was locked up..."

"From above!" answers Bodkin, dashing up the staircase. The friends arrive just in time to see the mysterious cloud beginning to rise with a rope ladder trailing down below it. Bodkin grabs hold of the bottom rung. "Stop!" he cries, but the next moment he is lifted off his feet and carried up into the air.

RUPERT

tries to help Bodkin

"Hold on tight!" the Professor calls -
Worried in case young Bodkin falls.

Jumping in the Professor's car
They hope the cloud won't travel far.

Then Bodkin disappears into
The cloud! Oh, no! What will they do?

The old man reaches out and flings
A lever and the car sprouts wings.

"Help!" wails Bodkin, but the cloud rises higher then starts to drift off across the fields. "Hold on tight!" calls the Professor. "We'll soon think of a way to get you down... Quick Rupert, the most important thing is not to let the cloud out of our sight." Hurrying downstairs, they run to the Professor's car.

To the pals' horror, Bodkin disappears inside the cloud. "It's getting away!" cries Rupert as the wind increases. "Not if I can help it!" declares the Professor, pressing a red button on the dashboard. There is a strange whirring sound from the front of the car...

RUPERT

sees a flying pirate ship

"What's happening?" gasps Rupert Bear.
"It's my invention, never fear!"

Now soaring up into the sky,
It's hard to believe what they spy.

A pirate ship soon greets their eyes -
With sails fluttering in the skies.

A look-out gives an urgent cry -
The ship speeds off into the sky.

"W...what's happening?" gasps Rupert. "It's my latest invention!" laughs the Professor as his car sprouts wings and soars up into the sky. The car speeds forward and is soon level with the strange cloud. Rupert peers ahead anxiously, then gasps aloud at the extraordinary sight that greets him...

"A flying pirate ship!" cries Rupert. Before he can say another word a pirate lookout gives an urgent cry and points towards the Professor's car. The ship's sails fill with wind and it starts to move away at top speed. "It's no use," says the Professor. "I can't go any faster. They're going to get away..."

The Old Prof. turns the car around
And lands it gently on the ground.

"Rupert!" he cries. "Those pirates bold
Were after my machine for gold!"

To PC Growler the friends go
And tell him of poor Bodkin's woe.

The policeman tells them to wait
The lure of gold will act as bait.

As they can't keep up with the ship, the chums go back to the tower where they hunt for clues to the pirates' raid. "Look at this!" cries Rupert. "They left a newspaper cutting all about your gold machine." "Of course!" says the Professor. "Gold! That's what those pirates are after..."

They decide to go and tell PC Growler the whole story. "Pirates!" exclaims the policeman. "Can't say we've had many of those in Nutwood lately..." He tells the Professor to go home and wait for the pirates to make their next move. "Bound to try again," he declares. "Pirates can't resist the lure of gold!"

Returning to the tower they're told:
"Pay for Bodkin with sacks of gold."

A note is left to show the place -
Where they must leave the ransom safe.

It's getting late and time to go
Back home. "I will let Growler know."

That night as he climbs into bed
An idea forms in Rupert's head.

Rupert and the Professor hurry back to the tower, where they find a message from the pirates pinned to the door. "They want us to give them Bodkin's weight in gold by noon tomorrow!" reads the Professor. "There's a map showing where we're to leave it – at the signpost by the Nutchester crossroads...

How dare they kidnap poor Bodkin!" he continues angrily. "You had better go home now Rupert, it's getting late. In the meantime I'll show this message to PC Growler..." That night, as he falls asleep, Rupert wonders how they can set Bodkin free. Suddenly, he has a brilliant idea...

RUPERT

helps make the gold

Next day Rupert runs all the way -
He has a plan to save the day.

Laughing - he tells of his great plan.
"The gold," he says. "Make all you can."

With whirring noise and flashing light
Out pour the coins all shiny bright.

"How marvellous!" young Rupert cries.
"The pirates won't believe their eyes."

Next morning, Rupert gets up early and hurries to see the Professor. "We've got to drive to the crossroads and leave as much gold there as we can!" he cries. "But!" the Professor protests, "if we did that the pirates would just load it aboard their ship and fly away..." "Not if my plan works!" laughs Rupert.

As soon as he hears Rupert's plan the Professor hurries to his workshop and switches on the gold machine. With a whirring of cogs and flashing of lights, it soon starts to make hundreds of shiny golden coins. "That's marvellous!" cries Rupert. "The more gold we can give those pirates the better...!"

RUPERT
carries the sacks

*The gold machine makes many loads -
For lots of trips to the crossroads.*

*The bulging sacks make quite a pile.
The pals hide out and wait a while.*

*The cloud appears just as foretold
And pirates start to load the gold.*

*The swag is loaded - they climb in.
Then, blindfolded, appears Bodkin.*

The gold machine mints so many coins that Rupert and the Professor have to make several journeys to the place marked on the pirates' map. By midday there is a large pile of bulging sacks at the crossroads. "That should do the trick!" says Rupert. The friends hide behind a hedge to watch...

Once more the dark cloud appears in the sky. As it hovers in the air a ladder is let down and two pirates start to load the sacks of gold into the ship. When the final sack has been carried aboard, the pirates clamber back and a third figure climbs slowly down the ladder. "It's Bodkin!" cries Rupert.

sets Bodkin free

While Bodkin frees himself of ties
The pirate ship takes to the skies.

"Look!" Rupert cries and all turn round -
The ship is heading for the ground.

The Professor acts without delay.
"We must not let them get away."

To the joy of our happy band
The ship comes crashing to the land.

Bodkin unties his blindfold and smiles happily. "That's better!" he cries. "Those pesky pirates made me wear this all the time! Their captain seemed afraid of being recognised." "Hmmm! I wonder," murmurs the Professor mysteriously. "Look!" cries Rupert. "The ship - it's starting to sink!"

"Quick!" cries the Professor. "We mustn't let them get away!" Although the ship is much lower in the sky, it still keeps sailing. "We'll soon see if your plan works," chuckles the Professor. The next minute the ship plummets down to earth with a loud bang...!

sees the ship sink

All the gold has turned to lead.
It's just as Rupert intended.

Police arrive upon the scene
To foil the robber pirates' scheme.

"Game's up!" calls Growler, and his team
Round up the gang of pirates mean.

The Prof. cries out: "Good work, my man!
I'm glad you followed Rupert's plan."

"W...what happened?" gasps Bodkin. "It's the gold!" explains Rupert. "They took so much, that when it turned to lead, the load became too heavy and the ship sank." As the pirates appear the friends hear a loud siren and see two police cars speeding towards the stranded ship.

Before the pirates can make a move PC Growler and a group of burly policemen leap out of the cars and move in to surround the entire gang. "Game's up lads!" calls Growler sternly. "Good work, constable!" cries the Professor. "I'm glad you got my message and followed Rupert's plan."

RUPERT

helps to capture the pirates

Says Growler: "What surprises me –
Where did they get the wizardry?"

"To learn to fly is quite a feat.
This scurvy lot aren't up to it!"

The Professor thinks there must be
Someone behind the trickery.

"Their leader still has not been found –
He is still on board I'll be bound!"

The captured pirates are led away towards the waiting cars by the policemen. "It puzzles me how such a gang of ruffians managed to make this boat of theirs fly," Growler says to Rupert and the Professor. "I've never seen anything like it!"

The Professor smiles. "There is someone else behind it all! Someone clever enough to build the flying ship. Someone cunning enough to plan the theft of the gold... And someone who has yet to give themselves up!" "Golly!" gasps Growler, "is their captain still aboard?"

"You've outsmarted me," moans a voice.
"I'm coming out – I have no choice."

"Doctor Brain! You're a clever man –
But to steal my gold was your plan!"

The handcuffed villain's led away
By PC Growler – what a day!

"I'll never mess with gold again,"
Says the Professor. "Nor will Brain!"

"Indeed," says the Professor. "You have outsmarted me again, Professor!" cries a voice from the ship. "Yes, Dr. Brain," says the Professor. "I guessed it was you when I saw the flying ship. You are a brilliant man, quite brilliant, but I know you cannot resist the lure of gold..."

"Hard to believe he's a pirate captain!" says PC Growler as he gets out his handcuffs to arrest Dr. Brain. "Oh, he's their leader all right," says the Professor. "But he's not the only one to blame. I'll know not to meddle with gold in the future..." "And so will Dr. Brain!" says Rupert with a grin.

THE END

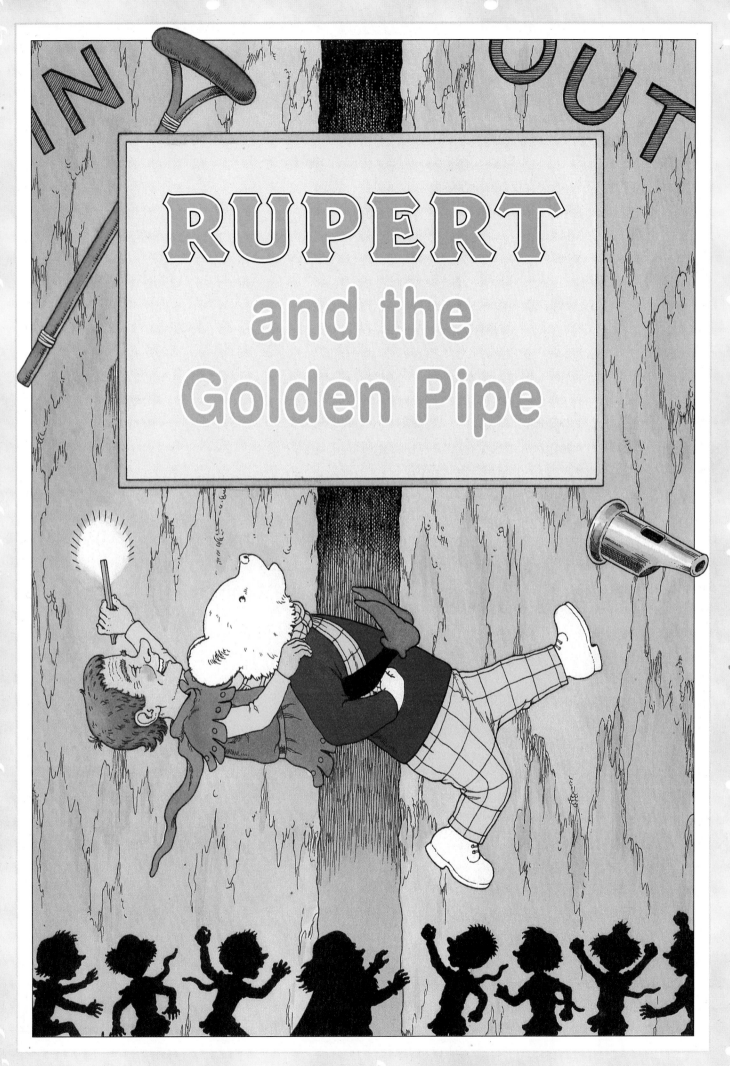

RUPERT
and the
Golden Pipe

RUPERT
decides to explore

"What a lovely day to explore,"
Thinks Rupert leaving his front door.

Then with a start he hears a sound -
Of whistling coming from the ground.

As he listens to the jingle
Both his feet begin to tingle.

"What is happening?" Rupert cries.
"'Tis my whistle," a voice replies.

Rupert has decided that it's just the sort of day to go exploring. He is in a part of Nutwood he doesn't really know and is wondering how much further he should risk going when he hears a faint whistling sound coming from somewhere nearby. To Rupert's surprise his feet start to tingle.

Rupert wonders if he has just imagined it, when again he hears the same musical whistling but this time it's much louder. Once more his feet tingle and then they start to move all by themselves... Suddenly a voice behind him says: "'Tis the wind blowing into my pipe that is making you dance!"

RUPERT

sees a golden pipe

There, sitting up against a tree
A little man. Who can he be?

"The pipe is magic. So your feet
Must dance to its music so sweet."

"I dropped it when I fell just now.
I'm hurt and just can't reach somehow."

"It's the same size as a pencil.
Please go and find it if you will."

There, sitting propped up against a tree, is a tiny man. "Gosh! Hello," gasps Rupert. "I saw how the music from my pipe was getting to your feet so I decided to speak up," says the stranger. Just then comes a puff of wind and with it the same whistling. This time Rupert finds himself almost jigging.

Luckily the whistling stops and Rupert's feet feel as if they belong to him once more. "Quick, get my pipe before it starts again," calls the little man. "It went flying when I tripped and hurt my ankle and I've not been able to get to it." Rupert turns to see a small golden pipe lying on the ground.

The pipe is not so hard to find.
"Just give it to me as it's mine!"

The little man lets out a yelp
And kind Rupert decides to help.

"I cannot walk," says the small man.
Says Rupert: "I'll help if I can."

"A piggy-back will do the trick
And get me home in just a tick."

Rupert picks up the little pipe and hands it back to its owner who tucks it safely into his belt. "Thank you so much," cries the little man. "You are kind...ooh!" His words give way to a groan. "My ankle really hurts," he explains. "I must try and help him," thinks Rupert.

"Can you walk at all?" Rupert asks. The man shakes his head sadly. "I must help you somehow," Rupert says. "But how?" "Well," says the other, "since I live not far from here and am not too heavy, maybe you could carry me home, give me what you people call a piggy-back?"

RUPERT

has to carry Trig

But Rupert's not too keen on this
Yet knows he must keep his promise.

Strangely the small man weighs a ton
To carry him will be no fun.

"My name is Trig. Let's start. Hooray!"
Then, puffing, Rupert starts to sway.

On his pipe Trig blows a jingle -
Rupert's legs begin to tingle.

This is a lot more than Rupert had bargained for but he can't back out now. "I'll be glad to," he says trying to sound as if he means it. "Kneel down and I'll climb on to your back," says the man. But, when Rupert gets to his feet, he finds that the stranger is very, very heavy!

"My name," says the little man, "is Trig." Rupert gasps out his name then attempts a wobbling step. "Which way?" he pants. "Just follow your feet!" chuckles Trig, and plucking the pipe from his belt blows into it. At the sound of the music Rupert's feet and legs start to tingle and jiggle.

RUPERT

dances over the ground

Trig's golden pipe gets one great blast
And Rupert's going very fast!

There is no chance that they will fall –
The man now weighs nothing at all!

"The land is rough but seems to be
As flat as a pancake to me!"

But suddenly Rupert's aghast -
He's running to a canyon vast!

The music from Trig's golden pipe grows faster, Rupert's feet start to move and away he skips. Now, though, Rupert finds an astonishing thing happening. Not only does Trig, who seemed so heavy, weigh nothing at all, but he himself is moving much faster than he can usually run.

No matter how rough the ground Rupert skips over it as if it were as flat as a pancake. "It's a great wee pipe this," Trig says. "You've only to know how many puffs to give it and it plays itself." Suddenly, to his horror, Rupert sees that they are heading straight for an enormous gorge!

RUPERT
is scared of the gorge

"Stop or we'll fall!" is Rupert's cry -
As with a toot they start to fly!

Then Rupert jumps with just one leap
Over the tumbling water deep!

But up ahead's a waterfall -
And no sign of Trig's house at all.

The water's spray wets Rupert's face
As onwards to the falls they race.

"Stop! We're going to fall," Rupert yells as his skipping feet teeter at the edge of the gorge. Trig chuckles and gives three sharp puffs into the pipe. Rupert's feet bound into action and he leaps effortlessly over the gorge to land safe and sound on the other side. "Soon be there!" cries Trig.

Rupert peers ahead expecting to see some sort of house or cottage but there's only a sheer cliff over which a waterfall is tumbling. Rupert is so close to the falls he can feel the spray. But there is no turning aside. For even above the roar of the water his feet can still hear the magic pipe.

RUPERT

skips up a cliff

Just as they are about to hit
The cliff, Trig plays just one more bit.

So Rupert finds that he can race
Up the slippery rocky face.

With Trig still high up on his back
They spot Trig's home just through a crack.

Trig puffs five times at a great rate -
The pillars turn and form a gate.

Just when one more skip would carry Rupert slap into the cliff, the pace of the music starts to race, and he finds himself dancing up the cliff face. At the top the pipe gives an extra trill and Rupert is upright again. Amazingly, he doesn't even feel dizzy. "There it is," Trig cries. "Right ahead."

The pipe music, back to its steady pace, carries Rupert and Trig up to a crack between two pillars of rock. Rupert hears Trig give five sharp puffs on the golden pipe. The pipe starts a new tune and the two pillars in front of them turn to make an opening in the cliff.

RUPERT

goes deep underground

"This is the In-World," Trig declares.
"Oh gosh! It's so dark!" Rupert stares.

But Trig plays on and forces him
To run into the tunnel dim...

Beyond the passage lies a cave
And happy Trig gives a big wave.

Trig's friends arrive - they look angry.
Whatever can the matter be?

"This is the doorway to In-World," Trig declares. "I...I'm not going in there," Rupert cries. But, when the music starts again, his feet begin to move and he is forced to run into the gloom of a long, dark passage. Behind him the door to the outside closes with a clang leaving only a small sliver of light.

A great cave lies beyond the passage. Growing down from its roof and up from the floor are what look like big stone icicles. "It's Trig, safe home but for a bit of a sore ankle!" Trig calls. Then from behind each "icicle" steps a little creature just like Trig, each carrying a tiny lantern.

*"I thought I would end up stranded!
I hurt myself when I landed."*

*But Rupert soon is filled with fear.
"What's that Out-Worlder doing here?"*

*"Rupert's the name of this stranger -
He rescued me from great danger."*

*But Magus says that Trig should not
Let strangers in. He'll go to court.*

The little creatures do not look very friendly. "I... I fell and hurt my ankle," stammers Trig. "I thought I was going to be stranded..." A little man, older than the others, steps forward and, pointing at Rupert, demands: "Who is that? Can it be you have brought an Out-Worlder here?"

"O, Magus," says Trig, "the stranger's name is Rupert and he has brought me home. I hurt myself and could not move..." Magus stops him with an angry cry: "You have sought help from one of the Out-Worlders. You know that is against our law!"

"Disgrace is brought upon you now."
"No!" answers Trig. "I'll tell you how!"

"I tricked that bear to carry me.
You should have seen me laugh. He! He!"

Magus is pleased to hear about
The trick. "Go on!" he gives a shout.

"A tale of great gold I did tell
And soon he fell under my spell."

Magus glares at Rupert and orders two In-Worlders to lift Trig down from his back. "Trig, you have brought disgrace on us by seeking an Out-Worlder's help," declares Magus. "No," Trig pleads, "I did not ask for help. I tricked this Out-Worlder into helping me." Rupert is shocked to hear Trig telling fibs.

"If you tricked him that may make a big difference," Magus tells Trig. "How did you do it?" Trig says that he told Rupert he was an elfin goldsmith and that if he carried Trig back home he would be given a fortune in gold. "Rupert was so greedy he said he would do it straight away," Trig cries.

Poor Rupert does not understand
Why Trig tells lies so underhand.

The In-Worlders are filled with glee
To see Rupert in misery.

To play a trick is fine by all.
"Well done young Trig! Rupert's a fool!"

Rupert is sad and sheds a tear.
"Please let me go. I must leave here."

Rupert starts to protest and says that Trig is not telling the truth. But he is shouted down and told to be quiet by the others. Rupert is so upset that he cannot speak and a tear starts to run down his face. However, the In-Worlders don't care and only laugh at him for having been so easily tricked.

Poor Rupert. He just can't understand creatures like the In-Worlders who think that trickery is good. Rupert is in tears and when at last the In-Worlders stop their nasty laughing, all he can do is sniffle and say: "You're horrible. I want to go home." At once there is silence.

is a prisoner

But Magus says he can't go home.
"You've seen our world. You may not roam."

"I won't tell!" pleads Rupert in fear.
"No!" says Magus. "You must stay here!"

"But," Rupert gasps, "that's just not fair.
Since I helped Trig get home back there."

"That's what you say!" they shout out loud.
But Trig's not joining with the crowd.

"Go home?" Magus cries. "Oh, no! You, an Out-Worlder, have seen our world. You cannot be allowed to return." "Oh, please," Rupert pleads, "I promise I shan't tell anyone that there's even such a place as this!" "The promises of an Out-Worlder mean nothing to us," Magus declares coldly.

Rupert can't believe this is happening to him. "It's not fair!" he bursts out. "I didn't want to come here. I only wanted to help." But the In-Worlders just make fun of him again. However, Rupert notices that Trig is not joining in. Maybe the little creature isn't quite as awful as he's seemed until now.

RUPERT

and Trig are left alone

Magus decides it's getting late.
"When we awake I'll choose your fate!"

"Trig will guard you well until then."
The pair are soon alone again.

Trig looks embarrassed and can't keep
His eyes open and starts to sleep.

"It's my duty to stay awake
Or Rupert Bear my pipe could take."

"Enough!" cries Magus. "Our sleep has been interrupted too long. Let us get back to our beds." He turns to Rupert. "I shall decide what's to be done with you later. Until then you shall stay here and Trig will guard you." With that Rupert and Trig are left alone.

Trig appears too embarrassed to look at Rupert. Then he yawns, leans back against a stony stump, shuts his eyes and starts to snore loudly. Rupert is much too worried to sleep. Trig begins to murmur as if talking in his sleep: "I must stay awake. If I don't, why, that little bear might take my magic pipe!"

Trig opens one eye - gives a wink.
"It's time to go, Rupert, I think."

"I'm sorry that I told a lie -
Now take the pipe, say Wheesht and fly!"

Smiling his thanks Rupert tiptoes -
Back to the entrance hall he goes.

He blows the pipe. He hears a yell.
"That bear has got my pipe as well!"

One of Trig's eyes opens. "They'll all be asleep by now," Trig whispers. "Take the pipe and go back to where we came from. When you get there say 'Wheesht' three times and leave the pipe there. I'll get it later. Now away – and I'm sorry I lied about you." Rupert smiles his thank you and tiptoes away.

Rupert creeps to the narrow strip of daylight which is the way out. He looks back at Trig, who is still pretending to sleep, and gives the pipe five hard toots! Everyone must hear! The doorway widens. Behind him Rupert hears Trig shouting: "My pipe! He's stolen it! He's getting away! After him!"

RUPERT

Trig is still making quite a din
As Rupert runs – they're after him!

Now Rupert stops and glances back.
Trig's sending them on the wrong track!

He gives the golden pipe some blows
And down the waterfall he goes.

Rupert skips to the pipe's new tune;
He's at the bottom very soon.

Heading for the waterfall Rupert risks a look back. Trig has pretended to stumble and is stopping anyone getting past him. He is also pointing away from Rupert and shouting: "There he goes! After the Out-Worlder!" Rupert grins only to find that he is almost on the edge of the waterfall cliff!

Just in time Rupert remembers to puff hard on the golden pipe! In an instant he finds that his feet are dancing down the cliff face only a short way from the tumbling water. When it looks as if he will hit the rocks at the bottom, the pipe gives an extra trill and he flips upright.

RUPERT

jumps the gorge

It looks as though Trig's saved the day
As Rupert's getting clean away.

He dances over ground quite rough.
Here comes the canyon...puff...puff...puff!

With tingling feet he has to get
Right to the spot where they first met.

He hides the pipe most carefully -
Then off he hurries for his tea.

Safely down the waterfall Rupert jigs away along the rocky bank. It looks as if Trig has managed to get the In-Worlders chasing the wrong way. The racing stream is cutting its way through steep rocky banks and Rupert knows he will be at the gorge soon. This time he is ready ... puff ... puff ... puff!

Rupert jumps the gorge easily and skips back to the place where he first met Trig. Reaching the spot, he says, "Wheesht" three times as Trig told him and at once the pipe is silent. He places the golden pipe as near as he can to where he found it. Then off he hurries to Nutwood and home.

At home he tells his Mum and Dad
Of the adventures that he's had.

"I think, " says Dad, "that you should stay
Away from that pipe when you play..."

In case the magic pipe he hears
He wraps his scarf about his ears.

The pipe has gone but Rupert blinks:
"I have a pal called Trig," he thinks.

Rupert's parents are amazed when they hear about his adventure with the In-Worlders. When Rupert offers to lead them to the golden pipe his Daddy says that it might be best if they stayed clear of the little pipe. "I don't fancy you being danced away by it again," he cries.

Some days later Rupert happens to chance upon the place where he left the golden pipe. He wraps his scarf about his ears so that he can't hear the music, but Trig has already taken the pipe. Although the In-Worlders seemed to be so awful, Rupert knows that at least one of them is his friend.

THE END

```
O B X C D P W Z P M
T M R T V O P Q L I
T Q U Z U D K B Y N
O E P O N G P I N G
L F E R D Y P N L F
I W R T X L K G L R
N U T W O O D O B E
E D W A R D M M I D
Q F Y G J I X B L D
F T I G E R L I L Y
```

1. RUPERT   7. PODGY

2. FERDY   8. BINGO

3. NUTWOOD   9. MING

4. EDWARD   10. FREDDY

5. OTTOLINE   11. BILL

6. PONG PING   12. TIGERLILY

Hidden in this wordsearch are names of some of your favourite characters and places. See if you can find them all. We've started you off by finding Rupert for you. Words may go across the page or down the page.   *Answers on page 109*

Spot the Difference

There are 10 differences between these two pictures. Can you spot them all? *Answers on page 109*

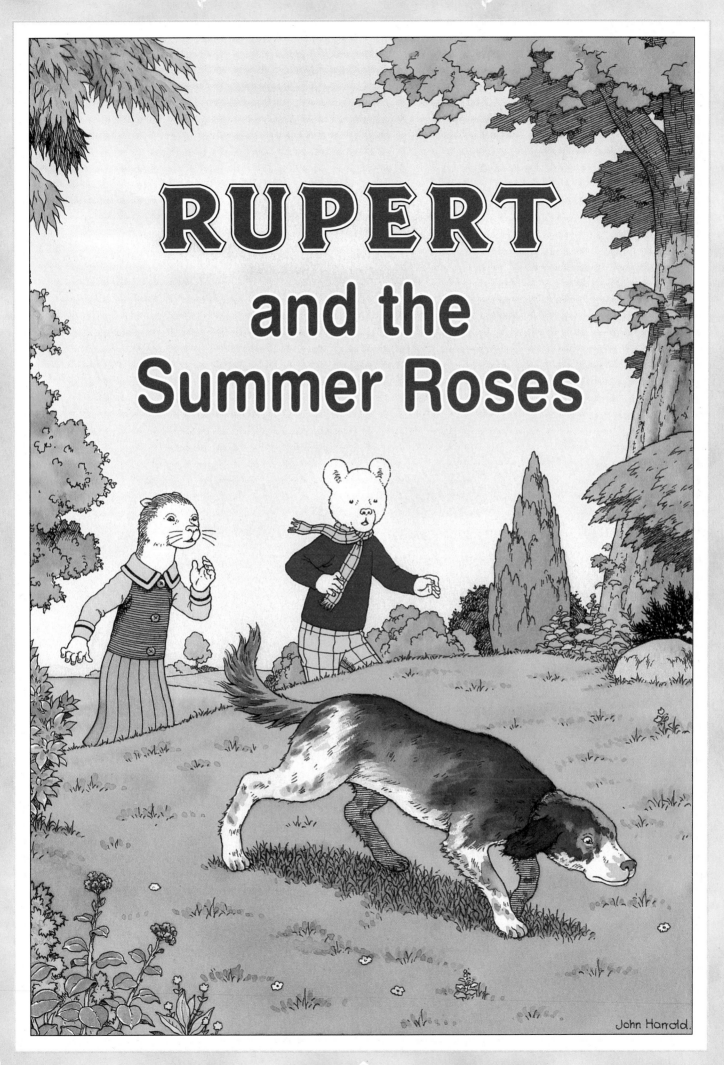

RUPERT
and the
Summer Roses

RUPERT
helps his Daddy

For Rupert's Mum a birthday treat,
He makes her buttered toast to eat.

Then Daddy thinks it would be fun
To pick a rose, "Just for your Mum."

In the garden goes Mr. Bear.
"I'll cut the nicest – that one there."

To his dismay it has no smell.
The others are the same as well!

Rupert and his Daddy are up bright and early, making a surprise birthday breakfast for Rupert's Mummy. Rupert is buttering the toast when his Daddy has a good idea. "Roses!" he cries. "Your Mum loves the smell of roses! We'll put one of her favourites on her breakfast tray..."

Rupert's Daddy leads the way to a tall rose bush, covered in beautiful flowers. He cuts a stem carefully, takes a deep sniff, then reels back in dismay. "No scent at all!" he gasps. "Try the others, Rupert..." Rupert sniffs one rose after another. Nothing! They're all the same...

RUPERT
hurries to meet Charlie

They choose a blossom anyway
And carry it upon a tray.

Mum thinks the rose is so pretty.
"No scent!" she sighs. "What a pity!"

Rupert says he's going to see
Charlie, Ottoline's new puppy.

Picking some flowers in the sun,
His friends are having super fun.

They decide to put the rose on the tray anyway, then march into the bedroom singing "Happy Birthday!" "How lovely!" says Mummy with a smile. "Thank you." "The rose is from the garden," says Rupert, "only it seems to have lost its scent..." "How strange!" says his mother, sniffing the flower.

With breakfast over Rupert hurries off to see Ottoline, explaining that she wants to show him her new puppy. He soon finds Ottoline picking flowers. "Hello!" she calls. "Come and meet Charlie! He's helping me choose the best flowers. Mother wants lots of lilies to put in the house..."

RUPERT
explains to Ottoline

He tells his chum that his don't smell.
"That is odd!" she cries "Mine as well!"

"Our lilies smell of lavender.
Which is so strange for a flower!"

A picnic is made by her Mum,
"Keep Charlie safe," she warns his chum.

Clutching the hamper and their tea,
The pair set off with the puppy.

"We've been picking my Mummy's favourite roses," Rupert tells his friend. "Only they've lost their scent." "That's odd!" says Ottoline. "Our roses don't smell of anything either, while the other flowers are all muddled up. The sweet peas smell of honeysuckle and these lilies remind me of lavender!"

Later on Ottoline's mother makes them a delicious picnic. "Remember not to let Charlie go wandering off. He doesn't know Nutwood yet and we don't want him getting lost!" she reminds them. When everything is ready, the chums set off for the common, carrying the hamper between them.

hears Charlie bark

They find a quiet and shady spot.
"Now, off you go and play!" says Ott.

Charlie starts barking by a tree.
"Come on!" says Rupert. "Let's go see."

"What's put him into such a state?
I suggest we investigate."

Something strange alerts their noses.
"Goodness! This bush smells of roses."

"This looks a good place!" says Rupert. "We can sit on the grass while Charlie has a run..." Suddenly they hear Charlie barking. "I wonder what he's found?" says Ottoline. The noisy puppy is standing in front of a bush barking and wagging his tail excitedly. Rupert and Ottoline decide to investigate...

"What's so special about this bush?" asks Ottoline. Rupert bends down to take a close look and suddenly understands why Charlie is so excited. "Roses!" he cries. "That's what's strange! The bush smells of roses, although there isn't a rose in sight..." "You're right!" gasps Ottoline. "I can smell them, too!"

RUPERT

follows the trail

Charlie moves on and wags his tail.
Cries Rupert: "He's picked up a trail."

Off though the wood the puppy goes
Following the scent with his nose.

Charlie stops eventually -
By the foot of an ancient tree.

A secret door is opening –
It's Sprig – a Nutwood Imp of Spring!

But Charlie has another surprise in store. As the chums look on, he sniffs the ground, then sets off across the common towards the woods. "He's picked up the trail!" cries Rupert. "Let's see where he goes." By the time the two pals catch up with him, Charlie has reached the edge of the woods...

Charlie has followed the rose-scented trail to the foot of a big old oak tree. Looking round to show what he has found, he wags his tail and barks loudly. Suddenly, a hidden door in the tree swings open and a scared looking figure peeps out. "It's Sprig, one of the Imps of Spring!" gasps Rupert.

RUPERT

meets an Imp of Spring

Says Rupert: "Sprig, it's only me!"
As Charlie jumps up playfully.

The Imp is scared of the puppy.
"Dogs like to chase us Imps you see."

Sprig explains it's his job to spray
Nutwood's flowers with scent all day.

"I'm busy at this time of year
With roses, lilies, lavender."

"Don't be frightened!" Rupert calls. "Charlie isn't as fierce as he sounds!" Charlie springs up, barking playfully. "Stop that!" says Ottoline. "Sprig is our friend. Sit down and be quiet." "Thanks!" says Sprig. "Dogs always make me nervous. They think it's good fun to chase us Imps through the forest."

Ottoline asks Sprig what he has been doing. "Imps look after all the gardens in Nutwood!" explains Sprig proudly. "My job is to give the flowers their perfume. I've been very busy what with roses and lavender to scent and everything coming into bloom at the same time!"

*Ottoline tells Sprig: "The trouble
Is your scents are in a muddle!"*

*"I dropped the tags!" he tells the pair
Holding his head in great despair.*

*"And then," he gulps, "the jars of scent -
I had to guess where each tag went."*

*"Tomorrow is Midsummer's Eve.
The day when Imps of Spring must leave."*

"Oh dear! You may have muddled things up!" laughs Ottoline. "The only scent of lavender in my garden is from the lilies." "Lilies!" gasps Sprig. "Oh no!" the Imp gulps. "Each flower has it's own scent bottle. And when I dropped the labels..."

"You put them on the wrong bottles," fills in Rupert. " Now all the flowers have the wrong scent!" wails the Imp. "What am I going to do?" Sprig tells them that the King is going to inspect the flowers: "This is my first year on the flowers. When His Majesty finds out what's happened, it will be my last!"

offers to help

*"The King will say the fault's all mine.
I've failed to scent the blooms on time."*

*"We'll help," the pair cry with a shout.
"We'll scent those flowers – there's no doubt."*

*"Come with me to the Imp's H.Q."
Says Sprig: "I'll show you what to do."*

*The chums clamber into the tree.
"This way," calls Sprig. "Just follow me."*

Sprig explains that it is Midsummer's Eve the next day. The time when the Imps hand over the management of Nutwood to the Autumn Elves. Everything has to be ready by then including the flowers! "How will I manage to spray them all again in time?" he says. "Don't worry," smiles Rupert, "we'll help."

Sprig decides to take Rupert and Ottoline to Imp Headquarters, where the scent is made. "But," he says, "Charlie will have to stay here as dogs are not allowed!" Stepping into the hollow tree, Rupert clambers down a flight of steps, which lead to a long underground passage. "This way!" Sprig calls. "Follow me..."

RUPERT

is shown the bottles

Sprig leads the friends deep under ground
To where his perfume workshop's found.

The workshop smells of strange flowers,
And labelling may take some hours.

Before the new perfume they spray,
They must wash the wrong scent away.

"How can we clean all the flowers?"
"I know," cries Rupert. "Spring showers!"

Sprig reaches a door marked "Perfumery." Stepping inside, Rupert can smell all sorts of different flowers, mixed up together, like a summer meadow... "This is where all the flower scents are made," the Imp announces proudly. "If you help me with the labels, we should be able to make up enough bottles..."

They soon manage to sort out the different flower scents. To Rupert's dismay, Sprig says they will have to give all the flowers a wash before they can be sprayed with the right scent. "That could take ages!" Rupert groans. He thinks for a moment, then asks Sprig if a heavy shower of rain might do the trick...

The Weather Clerk's asked if he could
Send lots of rain over Nutwood.

The Clerk says: "Of course, straightaway.
I'll send a rainstorm as you say."

Sprig gives the pals in a basket
The scents – as much as he can get.

As they run back to the old tree
The rain pours down quite merrily!

"Of course!" says the Imp. "Let's ask the Weather Clerk." He takes them to another room. Sprig pulls a lever, a screen set in the wall begins to glow and the Clerk's face appears. "Extra rain?" he laughs. "Most people ask for more sun! I'll send a fresh downpour to Nutwood straight away!"

Back at the workshop Sprig gives Rupert and Ottoline a basket each which they fill with lots of different scent bottles. As they head back to the tree trunk, Rupert hears the steady drumming sound of the Weather Clerk's rain overhead. "Goodness!" says Ottoline. "It's bucketing down!"

RUPERT

sprays the petals with scent

When the pals clamber from the tree
There's Charlie, waiting patiently!

As over Nutwood the friends go
In the sky is a great rainbow.

Rupert sees lots of blooms to spray.
"Gosh! Scenting will take me all day!"

"There's lavender and roses too -
Poor Sprig has loads of blooms to do!"

After a while the rain stops and, as the clouds clear, a brilliant rainbow fills the sky. The flowers have been washed clean of the wrong scent. Waving goodbye, the pals set off across the common, each in a different direction, ready to spray all the flowers with the right perfume.

Rupert sees lots of flowers on his way across the common. He sprays them carefully, one by one... "No wonder Imps are always busy," he thinks. "Their work's never done!" On the edge of the common, he comes to a clump of lavender, which he stops to spray. "I'll have to be sure nobody sees..."

Then, through a leafy arch of green
He spots a place he's never seen.

A rose garden with table low
And Ottoline who cries: "Hello!"

Roses seem to grow forever...
They decide to spray together.

Scenting the flowers is such fun.
Sprig laughs and says to them: "Well done!"

Setting off again, he spots a leafy archway and goes to take a closer look. "How odd!" he says. "I've never seen that here before!" Through the arch, Rupert comes to a wonderful rose garden, with a long, low table in the middle... The next moment Ottoline appears. "Hello!" she smiles, "isn't this lovely."

The garden is so full of roses that Rupert and Ottoline decide to spray them together. "Isn't it strange that we've never come across this place before?" says Ottoline. "Someone must have planted all these roses specially." "Excellent!" laughs Sprig as he joins them. "You have done well!"

The blooms are scented. All is done.
Cries Sprig: "To our grand feast please come."

Rose-dew he gives to Rupert and
Says: "For your Dad - a helping hand!"

Rupert is home in time to see
His Mummy have her birthday tea.

Under the cover of the night
The Imp's dew puts Dad's roses right.

Sprig tells them the rose garden is a secret meeting place for Imps and Elves. "Nobody knows it's here except for us!" he smiles. Thanking them for their help, Sprig asks them to come to the Midsummer Ball as his guests. Then he hands Rupert some rose-dew. "For your Dad's roses!" he says.

Rupert arrives home just in time for his Mummy's birthday tea. "Hello!" she says. "Did you have fun today?" "Oh, yes!" smiles Rupert. "We saw a rainbow, right over Nutwood!" That evening, Rupert slips out in to the garden with the rose-dew. He sprays each rose carefully, until they are all done...

Midsummer's Eve is here and so
To the great feast the chums must go.

Music plays out as they draw near
"Come on," cries Rupert. "Over here."

Sprig spots the pair and calls: "Hello!
Midsummer Eve is in full flow!"

"The flowers all smell sweet this year.
And so my work is finished here."

Next morning, Ottoline and Rupert go back to the rose garden where the Midsummer Ball is going to take place. "Isn't this exciting!" laughs Ottoline. As the chums approach the garden, they hear music playing. "The Ball must have already started!" says Rupert. "Let's go and see..."

Rupert and Ottoline find a crowd of Imps and Elves all chatting excitedly. "Hello!" calls Sprig. "I'm glad you could make it! Everyone has been saying how sweet the roses smell this year! I've finished all the gardens in Nutwood and now we can hand over to the Autumn Elves with everything up to date..."

RUPERT

meets the King of the Imps

*He takes them then to meet the King,
"My two helpers!" He gives a grin.*

*"Thanks to them both Our work is done.
Let's eat and drink and have some fun!"*

*Trumpets blast out a loud fanfare
As Elves take over Nutwood's care.*

*The pals then go back to the tree,
Where Imps may sleep quite happily.*

Sprig takes Rupert and Ottoline to meet the King. "These are my new helpers!" he announces. "Thanks to them, everything has been done on time." "Well done, all of you!" cries the King. "Our work is over for this year. Eat, drink and welcome to Rupert and Ottoline who are our special guests!"

There is a great fanfare of trumpets as the Imps' King hands his Chain of Office to the Chief Elf. "We entrust to you Nutwood as Summer turns to Autumn!" he declares. "Thank you!" replies the Elf. "We'll meet again at the start of Spring!" Then the Imps wave goodbye and go back to the hollow tree.

RUPERT
waves goodbye until next Spring

*Then through the secret door they go
To Imp H.Q. deep down below.*

*"See you next Spring!" the young Imp cries.
"We'll meet you here," Rupert replies.*

*Rupert gets home and his Dad's glad.
"The roses smell so sweet, my lad!"*

*They take the roses with perfume
To Mummy and scent fills the room!*

One by one, the Imps of Spring disappear through the secret door until Sprig is the only one left... "Goodbye!" he cries. "Thanks for helping! The King was so pleased he said that I could run the Perfumery next year, too!" "Good!" smiles Rupert. "We'll look out for you when Spring arrives..."

When Rupert gets home, he finds his Daddy, cutting more roses. "Hello Rupert!" he calls excitedly." The roses have got their scent back..." "Great!" smiles Rupert. "I'm glad the rose-dew worked." Rupert takes the roses to his Mummy. "What a lovely smell!" she cries. "It's filling the whole room..."

THE END

RUPERT and

*The chums are taking little Ming
On Nutwood Common out walking.*

Rupert, Bill Badger and Pong-Ping are taking Ming, the baby dragon, for a walk in the woods on Nutwood Common when they hear the sound of something crashing through the tops of the trees. "W... what's going on up there?" cries a worried Algy Ping. "A bird maybe," suggests Bill."No!" cries Rupert. "It's a hot-air balloon, and it's coming down fast!"

the Runaway Balloon

When suddenly they hear a sound -
A balloon's crashing to the ground!

Then, as he watches, Rupert sees
It getting stuck between the trees.

Rupert and the others can only stand and stare as the balloon crashes on through the trees. Something must be badly wrong with the balloon as it is losing height much too quickly. Luckily the balloon gets caught between the branches of two trees and touches down with only a small bump. The pals race towards the balloon as it comes to rest to see if they can be of any help.

Worried about the pilot's plight
Rupert calls out: "Are you all right?"

John Harold.

RUPERT

helps the balloonist

The balloonist answers: "Yes, thanks.
Just a problem with these gas tanks."

The little bear is quite confused:
"What are those burners that you use?"

"They heat the air and I fly high -
Can you help?" he asks with a sigh.

"For without heat it is no good -
I will be stranded in this wood."

"Are you all right?" Rupert asks the man in the balloon. "Yes, thanks," replies the balloonist cheerfully climbing from the basket as if crash landings were an everyday thing. "Sorry to drop in quite so unexpectedly. Fact is my burner packed up suddenly and I had no choice."

Rupert is puzzled and asks the man what a burner is. "It's a special machine which heats the air inside the balloon," the balloonist explains. "And because hot air rises it helps to make my balloon fly. Unfortunately my burner's broken. Do any of you know of someone who can help me?"

and Pong-Ping play a game

"The Professor will help I'm sure,"
Says Bill. "I'll take you to his door."

Rupert and Pong-Ping go to play
In the balloon without delay...

The chums are lookouts – pirating -
And do not notice baby Ming.

The little dragon plays a game -
Heating the air with his hot flame!

"The Professor," cries Bill. "Let me show you the way." The balloonist asks Rupert and Pong-Ping to look after his balloon. "But," he says looking serious, "please don't touch anything until I'm back." The pals can't resist though and before long they have climbed into the basket – just to see what it's like.

Rupert and Pong-Ping pretend they are pirates on a balloon journey. They get so caught up with their game they don't notice Ming scramble on to the burner ring. Ming is so excited by the balloon that he starts to breathe fire. Slowly the fire from Ming's breath starts to heat the air in the balloon!

RUPERT

is in a fix

*The balloon is filled and they rise
High into Nutwood's clear blue skies.*

*"Oh gosh!'" they cry as up they go -
The treetops are left far below.*

*The pals ask Ming: "Please don't stop now -
Without your air we'll crash somehow!"*

*Ming puffs hard and they fly higher.
Look! Up ahead there's a tower!*

As the balloon fills with hot air it begins to rise up off the ground. "What's happening?" gasps Pong-Ping. "We're going up," gulps Rupert, peering over the edge of the basket. "Help!" shout the pals. But by now it's too late. They are flying over the tree tops and still rising!

The chums are in an awful fix. What is the balloonist going to say? They don't want to crash so Ming is urged to keep breathing fire. The pals hope desperately that someone will see what's happening and come to rescue them. Just ahead they see the Professor's tower with a person on the roof.

RUPERT

waves for help

Bodkin looks skywards in surprise
And cannot quite believe his eyes.

Rupert and Pong-Ping wave and shout
But, oh no! Time is running out!

As higher in the air they float
They call for help from the Old Goat.

But sadly he seems not to hear.
Their flight continues – and their fear.

It's Bodkin, the Professor's assistant. He looks up in surprise as the balloon drifts past, but Rupert and Pong-Ping can't tell if he can hear their cries for help. He certainly waves back, but the wave could just be a friendly hello! Before the pals can do any more they are carried further away.

There's still one person who might be able to help them – the Wise Old Goat. The chums see him working in his garden and wave and shout to attract his attention but he shows no sign of having heard. They can only gaze back in dismay as they continue their flight to goodness knows where.

Rupert and Pong-Ping feel quite glum
As to tall mountain peaks they come.

Ming will run out of breath quite soon
And down they'll come in the balloon.

The flames from Ming are now so weak
They will soon crash upon a peak...

Then Pong-Ping calls out with a cry:
"This special fruit will help us fly!"

As Rupert and Pong-Ping watch the land below growing wilder something happens to give the pals reason to shiver. Ming leans down and chirps to Pong-Ping. "He's getting too tired to keep blowing flames," calls Pong-Ping. "He'll try to keep going but when he has to stop – down goes the balloon."

Ming's flames are growing weaker. Ahead of them rears an icy mountain which the balloon must surely crash in to. Then Pong-Ping gives a shout and plunges a hand into his pocket. He produces a round prickly thing like an un-peeled conker. "Dragon fruit. Let's hope I've remembered in time!"

RUPERT
and Pong-Ping crash land

*"The dragon fruit will boost young Ming
And to his breath hot fire will bring."*

*"That I had some I quite forgot -
But now Ming's flames are burning hot!"*

*Between great mountains the chums pass
Where lies a building made of glass.*

*Oh no, the pals are going to crash!
And to the ground they make a dash...*

Pong-Ping calls to Ming and feeds him the prickly dragon fruit. "Without this fruit dragons can't breathe fire," Pong-Ping tells Rupert. "I quite forgot I had one in my pocket." There is a whoosh from overhead and Ming breathes a strong jet of flame lifting the balloon over the snowy peak.

"Whatever is that?" says Rupert as they gaze down at a great glass building in the middle of the snow. Then he breaks off in dismay. The balloon is sinking fast. Ming has used up all the energy from the dragon fruit and has run out of flames. "Look out, we're going to crash!" Rupert cries.

is carried off

A snowy blanket saves their fall.
"Hooray! We are not hurt at all."

Rupert looks up - a man is there!
He seems quite scary to our bear.

Surrounded by the fallen snow
The pals are trapped, nowhere to go.

Picked up and tucked beneath each arm
Pong-Ping and Rupert feel alarm.

Just after Rupert's warning cry the balloon hits the ground. Luckily the snow is thick and soft for the pals are thrown out of the basket as it is dragged over. But, as they stand up, lumbering towards them is a huge figure in furs and dark goggles. "I don't like the look of this," quavers Rupert.

There's nowhere in this snowy waste for the pals to run to. The figure stops, fixes the pair with a dark-goggled stare, then, without a word, reaches out and tucks them under each arm. With Pong-Ping protesting loudly and the little dragon scampering behind, the figure makes for the building.

RUPERT

is taken to Mr. Jack

In the building they are taken -
Leaving the chums very shaken.

"To Mr. Jack you both must go -
Explain yourselves and what you know."

The trees and bushes on their route
Abound with massive, outsized fruit!

A man is standing with his back
Turned to the boys. It's Mr. Jack!

Rupert and Pong-Ping are carried into a small hall and put down. It's surprisingly warm after the bitter cold outside. They watch silently as the man takes off his fur suit and goggles. "Now," he says sternly, "you two are going to have to explain yourselves to Mr. Jack. He's not very keen on surprise visitors."

Rupert and Pong-Ping are led into a gigantic greenhouse. There are apples, pears, cherries, even bananas, all much larger and juicier than any they have seen before. When they reach a bed of giant strawberries they stop. In front of the strawberries, with his back turned towards them, is Mr. Jack.

He seems to be measuring the
Strawberries with a calliper.

"What are these strangers doing here?
No interruptions. Is that clear?"

"It was by accident we came
From Nutwood. Please let me explain."

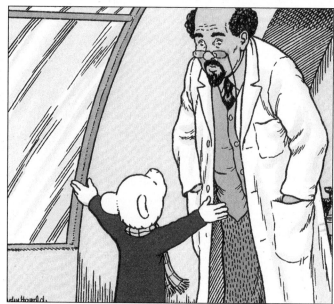

"My brother lives in your Nutwood -
Do you know him? I think you should!"

Mr. Jack is holding a quite enormous strawberry that he has been measuring with a pair of callipers. He stares at Rupert and Pong-Ping then he turns to the big man who is plainly his assistant. "Who are these children?" he demands crossly. "What are they doing here?"

"It's really too bad!" he continues. "I simply will not have children barging in here and interrupting my work!" "Oh, please, we meant no harm, sir!" stammers Rupert. "We were blown by the wind...all the way from Nutwood in a balloon!" At this Mr. Jack peers closely at Rupert.

"The Old Professor!" Rupert cries.
"He is my friend!" the bear replies.

"Let me see, now – we'll play a game.
Hmm! Rupert Bear must be your name."

"There is not much that I don't know -
I talk to all by radio."

"Let us call him and tell him how
You three are safe with me right now."

"Nutwood!" Mr. Jack exclaims. "My brother, the Professor, has lived there for years." "Gosh!" cries Rupert. "The Professor is my friend!" "Now then, let me see..." muses Mr. Jack. "Red jumper...yellow checked trousers...lives in Nutwood. Why, you must be Robert...no, Rudolph...no, Rupert Bear!"

"How do you know my name?"gasps Rupert in surprise. "Oh, my brother tells me everything that goes on in Nutwood," explains Mr. Jack, much happier now he knows who Rupert and Pong-Ping are. "We keep in touch by radio. In fact, let's call him now and tell him you are here safe and sound."

RUPERT
explores the greenhouse

Rupert cannot believe his eyes
And marvels at the fruits' great size.

Pong-Ping asks Jack about the heat -
To keep so warm must be a feat.

"I'll show you how!" the old man cries -
As down some stairs a hot spring lies.

"The air is heated and goes through
The building - that's what's warming you."

Mr. Jack leads the pals through the big greenhouse telling them about the special fruit he grows. "The result of years of experiments. The biggest and finest fruit anywhere." "How do you keep it so warm when you're surrounded by snow?" asks Pong-Ping. "I'll show you," says Mr. Jack.

A trapdoor reveals steep stairs down to a brightly-lit cave. Steam rises from a stream running through. "It's hot!" gasps Rupert as they make their way beside the stream. "A thermal spring," says Mr. Jack. "It heats the glasshouse, and when it's cooled provides water for the plants."

tries to radio Nutwood

Into the study they all go
And hurry to the radio.

It crackles – there's a faint voice too!
"Hello Nutwood – I can't get through!"

"They will all worry about us!"
Says Rupert. "There will be a fuss!"

"We'll find some dragon fruit for Ming.
And once again you'll be flying."

When they get to Mr. Jack's study he tries to call the professor on the radio. But all that comes from the speaker is a loud crackling over which they can just make out a faint voice saying: "Not here. He's ..." "Bother!" cries Mr. Jack. "I can't get through when it's like this. Sorry."

"We must get back," groans Rupert. "My parents will be worried." "Perhaps if we had more dragon fruit..." ventures Pong-Ping. "Why dragon fruit?" asks Mr. Jack. Pong-Ping tells how Ming helped the balloon fly but needs dragon fruit to make flames. "I think I can help," cries Mr. Jack. "Follow me."

He takes them to a dragon tree.
They pick as much as they can see.

They feed the dragon fruit to Ming,
And wonder if the wind's blowing.

To check the breeze the pals must go.
So wrap up warm against the snow.

Testing the wind they scan the skies -
In the distance is a surprise.

When Mr. Jack told them that he had "the finest fruit" in his greenhouse, neither pal thought that included dragon fruit. But it does! Pong-Ping feeds one to a delighted Ming. When they have gathered enough to keep Ming breathing flames for a long time, Mr. Jack suggests getting back to the balloon.

The assistant opens the main door and out they go on to the snow. Mr. Jack holds up a hankie to test which way the wind is blowing. Until it is blowing towards Nutwood a return balloon flight is impossible. Suddenly Rupert spots something rise above the peaks. "It's another balloon!" he cries.

The Old Professor and his chum -
The pilot - who thought he might come.

The friends are welcomed with a cheer.
"Hello!" they cry. "We're glad you're here."

"When Bodkin saw you flying past -
Into my balloon we jumped fast."

"We guessed that you had broken free
So flew on to where you might be."

There, waving from a gas propelled balloon are the Professor and the balloonist. "Well, well, well, who would have thought ..." Mr. Jack keeps repeating as the pals run to greet their friends. "We're sorry we took your balloon," they gasp to the balloonist. "We should have done what we were told..."

Back in Mr. Jack's study the Professor explains it was no radio call that had brought them. "We must have left by the time you called," he says. "When Bodkin said he'd seen you fly past we guessed what had happened. So we took off in my two-seater and let the wind carry us here as it did you."

"Now off to Nutwood - no delay!"
But the wind's blowing the wrong way...

"There is no need to worry though
With my balloon I'll give a tow."

The balloonist thinks that Ming is great.
"I'll take him home. He is first rate!"

"Just joking!" he informs the pair,
As Pong-Ping gives an angry stare.

"Now, we must set off for Nutwood at once," the Professor tells the pals. "Everyone is worried about you." "But isn't the wind blowing the wrong way?" Rupert protests as they follow the Professor towards the main door. "I can use my engine to tow you if it's not too strong," is the reply. "Come on!"

The balloonist and Ming hurry ahead to inflate the balloon. It's ready in no time thanks to Ming's fiery efforts. "I say," chuckles the balloonist, "this little chap is just the right sort of pet for someone like me!" Then seeing Pong-Ping's outraged expression, adds hurriedly, "Only joking, you know!"

RUPERT

is happy to be back

Tied together by a strong rope -
They're going home full of new hope.

Back over mountains high they go.
"Goodbye!" they wave to those below.

"Look!" Rupert calls. "There's Mum and Dad."
To see him they are very glad.

He gets a hug from his Mummy
And Dad, and now it's time for tea.

A towline is tied between the balloons and the two crafts start to rise. When the Professor thinks they are high enough, he gives a thumbs-up signal, switches on his engine, waves goodbye and off they go. Flying over Nutwood they even see the Wise Old Goat who looks up and waves.

"Look, there's Mummy and Daddy!" cries Rupert. The Professor thinks they must have been waiting a long time. "I sent Bodkin to tell them what happened, and that we'd gone to rescue you." A few minutes later, Rupert is rushing forward to be hugged by a delighted Mummy and Daddy.

THE
END

Can you join the dots to see who is hiding? *Answers on page 109*

Now you can colour them in.

RUPERT
and
the Screen

John Harrold.

Rupert has said that he would stay
At Tigerlily's house today.

He takes delivery of a gift
So big it takes two men to lift.

Into the study they must go.
"What is inside?" They want to know.

A lovely Oriental screen -
The like of which they've never seen.

Tigerlily and her Daddy, the Conjurer, are going to Nutchester for the day. The Conjurer is expecting a parcel to arrive and Rupert has volunteered to stay in the house until it comes. They have not been gone for long when a van draws up and two men unload a mysterious looking package.

Rupert tells them to put the package in the Conjurer's study and leads the way there. "Like us to set it up for you?" the men ask helpfully. "Yes, please," Rupert says. The wrappings are taken off and a beautiful oriental screen is revealed. Their work done, the two delivery men take their leave.

RUPERT
opens a secret door

As it is placed upon the floor
Rupert detects a hidden door.

He turns the handle with a click.
The door swings open – what a trick!

Before him lies a country scene -
With bright blue skies and fields of green.

He dashes round the Eastern screen
But there is nothing to be seen.

As Rupert is looking at the elaborate carving on the screen he spots a small door in the central panel. "It looks so real!" he thinks and takes hold of a carved flower in the middle of the door. To his surprise the flower turns with a sharp click and the door swings open...

Rupert peers through the tiny doorway and gasps with surprise. He sees before him a vast expanse of beautiful countryside! He can even smell fresh air and feel a warm spring breeze. "Impossible!" thinks Rupert and he hurries round to check the other side of the screen. There is nothing to be seen.

RUPERT

is being watched

Rupert is curious to know,
So through the door he thinks he'll go.

A short dark tunnel leads our bear
Into a land beyond compare.

Grassy banks and a crystal stream.
Rupert gasps - he is in a dream.

"How wonderful – how clear the skies!"
But turning, he feels someone's eyes.

Rupert goes back to take another look through the little door. The countryside is still visible, and the longer he looks at it, the lovelier it seems. Without thinking what he is doing, he squeezes through the doorway. It is just big enough for Rupert, but no grown-up could ever fit through.

"Wherever this place is, it's lovely," thinks Rupert. The air is full of the freshest scents. A crystal stream runs between smooth grassy banks speckled with flowers. A kingfisher darts along a stream. "How wonderful!" he sighs. All of a sudden, Rupert has a strange feeling that he is being watched.

Then, in the quiet, he hears the sound
Of feet crunching upon the ground.

"Come out!" he calls. Then round a tree
A boy appears: "You'll not take me!"

But Rupert does not understand
The boy and asks him: "Where's this land?"

"This is the Other Land you see
There's only you in here – and me!"

Then he hears the unmistakable sound of a twig being snapped underfoot. "Come out!" calls Rupert. "I know you're there!" From behind a tree, a young boy steps out. Before Rupert can say anything, the boy cries: "You are from my master, aren't you? Go back. Tell him I shall never return!"

Rupert stares at the boy. "I've no idea what you are talking about!" he says. "Do you know what this place is?" "This is the Other Land," the boy stammers uncertainly. "Is there anyone else here?" asks Rupert. "Only me," the boy sighs. Then, brightening up, he adds: "And you as well, of course!"

RUPERT
meets Samu

"My name's Samu. I was a slave -
A sorcerer's." The boy looks grave.

"He sent me through a hidden door
And now I'm here for ever more."

Rupert cries out: "I know that way-
I came through the same door today."

"Come back with me to Nutwood where
It's safe. He will not find you there!"

"My name is Samu," the boy continues. "I was apprentice to a wicked sorcerer who used me as a slave. One day, he bought a screen with a secret door. He was too big to fit through the doorway, so he sent me instead. It was then I saw my chance to escape. And I did which is why I am here..."

"Gosh!" cries Rupert. "I came here through the same door as you." "Then you are from my master!" Samu hisses. Rupert explains about the screen being delivered to the Conjurer's house. "You could go back through it quite safely now," he says. "Never!" says Samu. "It is a cruel world out there!"

RUPERT

is lost

Samu says "No!" But wants to show
Rupert the land he's come to know.

Rupert agrees reluctantly
For back in Nutwood he should be.

"Wait just a moment," says Samu.
"There is one more place you must view."

Leading the way Samu strides on...
Then off he runs! Where has he gone?

Rupert knows he should really return home without delay but Samu wants to show him something of the Other Land and he agrees to take a quick look round. Samu explains that his drinking water comes from a spring, while his food grows on the luscious nut and fruit trees that grow overhead.

"I must be getting back now," says Rupert. "Wait!" cries Samu. "There is one more place for you to see." Rupert agrees and the pair set off. The way seems to twist and turn so much that Rupert is soon lost. Suddenly Samu darts off among the trees and disappears from sight...

*"Come here!" calls Rupert, but Samu
Has disappeared. What will he do?*

*Rupert must get back home somehow -
But which way should he go right now?*

*He climbs atop the tallest tree.
"Where can the path we just took be?"*

*"Oh good! There is the stream I saw -
It flows beside the magic door."*

"Come back!" calls Rupert. But Samu does not come back. "I must get home," thinks Rupert. "But which way? I'm quite lost ... perhaps if I keep climbing to the top of this hill I'll be able to see the way from there." Rupert clambers up, but he finds the trees are too thick to see anything.

"I'll just have to climb to the top of the tallest tree," he thinks. When he gets there, Rupert finds he can see all around but there's still no sign of the path. Then far off he spots the stream that runs beside the magic screen. Rupert scrambles down and sets off through the forest.

RUPERT
hears his name

*He hurries down between the trees
And finds the path – Rupert is pleased.*

*He runs to where he left the screen –
Between two rocks it lies hidden.*

*From deep within the darkness black
He hears a voice: "RUPERT! Come back!"*

*"Don't go!" cries Samu suddenly.
"I need you here. Please stay with me."*

As Rupert hurries down to the stream he notices that, despite all the trees, he can just about follow a straight line. Samu had meant to confuse him with all the twisting and turning on the way up! At last he sees the tall rocks he passed between after coming through the screen.

Rupert peers nervously into the shadows behind the rocks. It is very dark inside. "RUPERT!" Rupert jumps as from deep within the shadows he hears his name. "I...Is that you, Samu?" he quavers, tiptoeing forward. "Don't go! Stay here!" Rupert swings round to see Samu just behind him.

RUPERT
feels sorry for Samu

"I'll be so lonely without you!"
Weeps the poor boy. "What will I do?"

"RUPERT!" Again his name's called out.
"I'm coming!" Rupert gives a shout.

Though Rupert's sorry for Samu -
He wants his Mum and Daddy too.

So Rupert asks the weeping lad
To come home with him, "Don't be sad!"

"Why did you play such a mean trick on me?" asks Rupert. "I didn't want you to go," Samu says sadly. "I'm lonely and I wanted you to stay..." Rupert feels sorry for Samu even though the boy was ready to stop him getting back home. "RUPERT!" the voice from the shadows calls again.

Rupert starts walking towards the voice. "Please don't go!" begs Samu. "But, I want to go home!" says Rupert. Ahead of him the voice cries: "Now I see you! Keep going. It is I, the Conjurer." Rupert laughs with relief. Then he stops and turns back to Samu. "Will you come with me?" Rupert asks.

RUPERT

and Samu go back

"But I tricked you!" cries young Samu.
Smiles Rupert: "I've forgiven you."

Then Rupert sees beyond the door
His friend the Chinese Conjurer.

Rupert takes Samu by the hand
And leads him out of Other Land.

They meet the Conjurer who knew
Of Samu's evil master too!

"Even though I tricked you?" quavers the boy. "Only because you were frightened of being left alone," Rupert says. "Who is that with you?" the Conjurer calls. "A new friend," Rupert replies. "He's coming too." Rupert bends down to find himself face to face with the Conjurer!

Rupert and Samu squeeze through the screen door to be greeted with wide smiles by the Conjurer and Tigerlily. The Conjurer apologises for not warning Rupert that the screen was magic and listens carefully as Samu tells his story. "I knew your evil master!" the Conjurer declares.

learns that Samu is free

"His cruelty's too hard to bear,"
Gasps Samu. "Please don't send me there!"

The Conjurer says: "Do not fear
The Magician's gone far from here."

Asks his daughter Tigerlily:
"Can Samu work for you Daddy?"

The Conjurer shakes his wise head:
"My friend needs Samu's help instead."

"Don't make me go back to him!" gasps Samu. "No," says the Conjurer gently, "I would never do that. He was a wicked man." "Was?" Samu repeats. The Conjurer nods: "He lost a battle of spells to a magician friend of mine and disappeared in a puff of smoke! I was sent his screen as a gift!"

Samu is finally free of his wicked master! "Daddy," says Tigerlily, "might you take Samu as an apprentice now that he is free?" The Conjurer shakes his head. "No, daughter," he says. "But, I will find a new and kind master for him among my magician friends." The chums clap their hands with glee.

RUPERT

sees the screen leave Nutwood

"I'd love to visit Other Land,"
Sighs Tigerlily. "It sounds grand!"

"You may get lost – you must not know
The Other Land. That screen should go!"

A large parcel makes Rupert stare -
The magic screen is packaged there.

"Museum of Magic," reads the bear
And "To be sent – with utmost care!"

At tea, Tigerlily's eyes sparkle as Samu describes the beautiful trees and flowers that grow in the Other Land. "How I'd love to visit it!" she says. "No!" cries her father, leaping to his feet. "You might get lost and never find your way back. That screen is dangerous. I must find another home for it."

Later that week Rupert is at Nutwood station and sees the delivery men carrying a familiar package. "The Conjurer didn't keep this long," says one. Rupert reads the label on the parcel: "To the World Museum of Magic with utmost care." "I'm sure that's the safest place for it," he thinks.

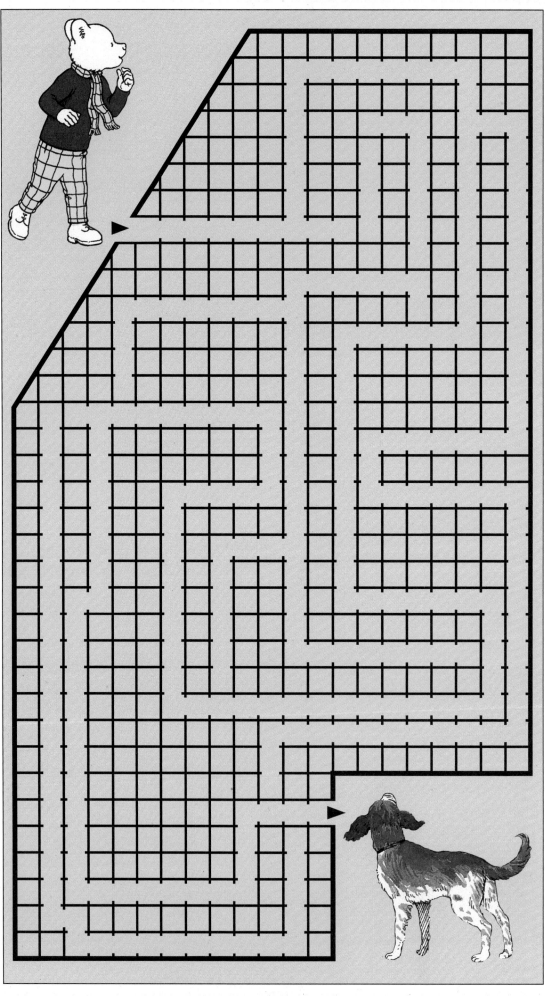

Can you help Rupert find Charlie? *Answer on page 109*

Q. Why did the pony cough?
A. He was a little hoarse!

Q. What do dogs eat at the cinema?
A. Pup-corn!

Q. Why couldn't the bicycle stand up?
A. Because it was too tyred!

A RIDDLE FOR YOU TO TRY
Q. What never gets any wetter, no matter how much it rains?
A. The sea!

Q. Why was the broom late?
A. It over swept!

Q. What do you call a sleeping bull?
A. A bulldozer!

Q. What is a duck's favourite television show?
A. The feather forecast!

Knock, knock!
Who's there?
Cows
Cows who?
No they don't, they moo!

Knock, knock!
Who's there?
Boo
Boo who?
Don't cry, it's only a joke!

Q. What do you give a sick pig?
A. Oinkment!

Christmas Crackers...

Knock, knock!
Who's there?
Avery
Avery who?

Avery merry Christmas!

Q. What did the big cracker say to the little cracker?

A. My pop's bigger than yours!

Q. What's brown and sneaks around the kitchen?

A. Mince spies!

Q. What do snowmen eat for lunch?

A. Iceburgers!

Q. How do chickens dance at the Christmas party?

A. Chick to chick!

Knock, knock!
Who's there?
Mary
Mary who?

Mary Christmas!

RUPERT and

It's Rika's job throughout the year
To care for Santa's flying deer.

Between Christmases Santa's reindeer are cared for by a girl named Rika at her home in Lapland. On her way there Rika often visits Nutwood to see Rupert. Since Santa doesn't like his reindeer to be seen by too many people they are flown in and out by night and kept in the large, very private garden of Rupert's chum, Pong-Ping. This year Rika is later than usual as she has been helping Santa to tidy up.

John Harrold.

the Reindeer Rescue

If Rika visits Rupert then,
She hides them in Pong-Ping's garden.

This Christmas Rika's asked to stay
By Rupert's Mum – just one more day.

For one reason and another Rika has never had a real chance to see Nutwood properly. So this year Rika is delighted when Rupert's Mummy asks her if she would like to stay an extra day, and heads off with Rupert to ask Pong-Ping if he'd mind having the reindeer just a bit longer. Pong-Ping's a good pal, the reindeer seem happy and so, of course, he agrees at once.

Pong-Ping is pleased and says he'll keep
The reindeer safe where they can sleep.

RUPERT

talks about Sir Jasper

On the way home a country pile
Has leading to it a small stile.

"A shortcut can't do any harm."
"Oh no!" cries Rupert in alarm.

To Nutwood Court belongs the ground
Where once poor Rupert had been found.

"Keep out and don't come back at all!"
Rupert was told by Jasper cruel.

See you tomorrow night," says Pong-Ping. The pair set off for Nutwood village. As they go around the woods of a large estate Rika suggests they take a shortcut through the grounds. "See, there's even a stile," she says. "Oh no!" cries Rupert in alarm. "Why?" Rika asks. "What's so awful in there?"

"Those woods belong to Nutwood Court," explains Rupert looking frightened. "For a long time it was empty and I used to use it as a short cut. One day a man grabbed me, said I was trespassing and marched me before the owner, Sir Jasper. I was let go providing I never came back. But I did..."

hears a scuffle

But back he came and helped to save
A baby yeti caught enslaved.

"Sir Jasper is so cross with me!
Since Little Yum we set quite free."

Then suddenly they hear a shout -
Whatever is that noise about?

Freddy and Ferdy have been caught
By Scrogg: "A lesson you need taught!"

"I went back with Pong-Ping," Rupert continues. "Sir Jasper is a trapper of rare animals and he had caught a baby Yeti called Yum. We helped to free Little Yum and Sir Jasper is still angry with me...!" Rupert shivers. All of a sudden they hear the sound of a scuffle and wailing coming from the woods.

The shouting is being done by someone Rupert knows only too well – Sir Jasper's henchman, Scrogg. Wriggling and wailing in his beefy grasp are the Fox brothers, Ferdy and Freddy. "You'll be for it from Sir Jasper!" Scrogg bellows. "He hates nosy parkers..." He looks up: "You!" he snarls at Rupert.

Scrogg spots Rika in her strange gear.
His look fills Rupert with great fear.

'Run!" Rupert cries. "Find help somehow."
But Scrogg is asking questions now.

"The Foxes know about your deer."
Then running hard they both appear.

Rika's puzzled: "He's set them free!
Whatever can the reason be?"

"We'd better get help," says Rupert, and he starts to move away. Scrogg stares at Rika and at her Lapp clothes. Rupert tugs Rika's hand and she hurries away with him. When Rupert glances back Scrogg is pointing after them. Plainly he is asking about Rika and, anxious to please him, the pair are talking.

Rupert is very worried since the Fox brothers know all about Rika and the reindeer. Just then there is a scampering and the Foxes appear, running hard. "That man must have let them go!" exclaims Rika. "I wonder why." Rupert has a feeling he knows the reason – and he doesn't like it at all.

"What did you say to Scrogg back there?"
Asks Rika of the shifty pair.

"Oh, just about your reindeer and
Where they're staying on Pong-Ping's land."

Then hand in hand the two take flight.
Says Rupert: "You must leave tonight."

"Or Scrogg will try to steal, I fear,
For Jasper, Santa's flying deer!"

"Out of our way!" pants Freddy. "Not before you tell us what you told Scrogg," says Rika. "He said not to tell," Ferdy cries out before Freddy can stop him. "You'd better or Santa will hear of this and you'll be in trouble," Rika says grimly. "Oh, it was just about you and your silly reindeer," Ferdy mumbles.

Suddenly Freddy grabs Ferdy's hand and the two race away. "We must get home and tell Mummy you are going to have to leave tonight," Rupert gasps. Rika stares at him. "Don't you see? Scrogg will tell Sir Jasper about your reindeer and he'll try to steal them. What a prize for him! Flying reindeer!"

RUPERT

gets the reindeer ready

*Rika cries: "They wouldn't dare to
Steal from Santa. That just won't do!"*

*But she decides to get away -
And packs her bag without delay.*

*Later that night all's ready, so,
To fly to Lapland they must go.*

*Then from the shadows comes a voice.
It's Growler – though he has no choice.*

"That Sir Jasper wouldn't dare!" cries Rika. "He would!" declares Rupert. "He'll try one way or another." "Then I must get the reindeer away as soon as I can," Rika says. "We shall have to wait 'til dark, though." And so, a little later, Rupert's Mummy is helping Rika to pack.

The moon is bright over Pong-Ping's garden. Rika and the reindeer are ready to go. Rika is giving Pong-Ping a farewell hug when from the shadows a voice rasps: "Officer, do your duty!" Into the moonlight step Scrogg, Sir Jasper and Nutwood's policeman, PC Growler, who is plainly very embarrassed.

*"Err, I've been told by Jasper here
That you have brought in flying deer."*

*"It's not allowed so you must go
Back to my Station, don't you know."*

*Says Jasper slyly: "I'll help you.
Just put the reindeer in my zoo."*

*But PC Growler tells him: "No!
With me these animals must go!"*

"Young miss," says PC Growler. "It has been brought to my notice by Sir Jasper here that contrary to the law you have brought into the country four flying reindeer." Rupert stares in disbelief at Growler. "Go on!" Sir Jasper hisses. Growler sighs: "Therefore, you and the animals must go to prison."

"I'll look after the reindeer for you, officer," Sir Jasper says smoothly. "I have plenty of space at my zoo." "No!" Growler declares. "The law you so kindly drew my notice to says they must go to jail. So they are all coming with me!" Scrogg and Sir Jasper glower at Growler.

RUPERT

hears Rika crying

Sir Jasper's cross – he's coming too.
He wants those reindeer for his zoo!

The group set off without a sound -
To Nutwood Station they are bound.

Poor Rika's crying before long
And Growler thinks that it's all wrong.

So muttering, he winks his eye
And asks: "How do your reindeer fly?"

"Right, miss, mount up," Growler tells Rika. "You too, Rupert. Pong-Ping can stay here." "We are coming too, to see that everything is done properly!" snaps Sir Jasper who is not going to give up so easily. "As you like, sir," Growler says. In silence the group set off towards Nutwood Police Station.

Sniff! Sniff! Rupert sees that Rika is crying. Growler hears the crying as well and mutters what sounds like: "This is all wrong!" Then he asks Rika a very odd question: "Miss, I've been wondering, how do you get those reindeer of yours to fly?" Rupert stares at Growler who very slowly winks at him.

"Why is Growler behaving so?"
Thinks Rupert. "Gosh! Maybe I know!"

"He's going to let us all go free!"
And winks at Rika secretly.

Young Rika shouts out "Hop Ol Hai!"
To make the captured creatures fly.

Three reindeer bound up in the air -
But one is trapped by the sly pair.

Rupert feels sure Growler is trying to help Rika. So, with a wink, Rupert prompts her as well: "Go on, Rika. Tell PC Growler how you get the reindeer to fly." Growler has raised his helmet to scratch his head and let go of the reindeer. "I say 'Hop Ol Hai'," she grins. "Pardon?" asks Growler.

"Hop Ol Hai!" Rika repeats. "Hop Ol what?" Growler asks, cupping an ear. "HOP OL HAI!" she shouts. At once three of the reindeer bound into the air with Rupert holding on tight. But Scrogg and Sir Jasper are holding the last reindeer down and not letting it go. "We must go back!" cries Rika.

"Give me that deer - right now, please, Sir!"
Says Growler to the cross Jasper.

He takes the reins, cries "Hop Ol Hai!"
And flies the deer high in the sky.

They wait until they have some height
And grumpy Jasper's out of sight.

Growler says that they must land - so
Down to the ground the fliers go.

"No! Go on!" shouts Rupert. "It'll be all right!" Sure enough PC Growler has raced over to Sir Jasper and is shouting, "In the name of the law, release that reindeer. I need it to give chase!" He grabs the reins, jumps on the reindeer's back, shouts "Hop Ol Hai!" and is carried high into the air.

"Go slowly enough to let PC Growler catch up once those baddies can't see us," Rupert calls. The reindeer slow and Rika keeps them just high enough to clear the tree tops so that they'll be hidden from view. "Land at once!" shouts Growler, pretending to look fierce. "Ol Lo!" cries Rika.

They land and Growler gives a yell
To Rupert, "Please get down as well!"

So that Rika can get away -
Growler climbs off, pretends to sway.

"Oh goodness me! What's happening?
Come back!" calls Growler with a grin.

Rika blows him a goodbye kiss.
Says Growler: "What a saucy Miss!"

The reindeer land on a lonely stretch of open country not far from Nutwood. "Rupert, get down at once!" cries Growler. He then pretends to fall off his reindeer and stumbles towards Rika. "As for you, miss, and your Hop Ol whatsit...!" Rika grins at Growler and calls back, "What you mean is – Hop Ol Hai!"

At Rika's cry all her reindeer bound into the air. "Come back here!" croaks Growler. "Gosh! What a time to lose my voice!" he grins. "It's all this shouting in the cold night air." Rika waves goodbye – and blows a kiss to Growler. "What a sauce!" he says – with a big smile on his face.

RUPERT
watches Growler fall over

So the reindeer for ever more
May come back - he will change the law.

Then with a smile he pretends that
He has tripped over his hat!

Quickly Rupert runs up to care -
Poor Growler looks the worst for wear!

"Oh, well!" grins Growler. "But I fear
You do get dirty chasing deer!"

"Oh dear! Will Rika ever be able to come back?" Rupert asks anxiously. "Sure of it," Growler says. "By next Christmas the rules will be changed so that they don't apply to reindeer. I'll make certain of that." Suddenly Growler trips, drops his helmet and falls on it. "Oh, it's not my night!" he chuckles.

"Are you all right?" Rupert cries in dismay. But Growler doesn't seem to he hurt. Though his helmet does look the worse for wear. "Oh, well," grins Growler, "I suppose you must expect to get a bit crumpled if you fall off a reindeer. But it will show Sir Jasper I did my best to try and catch young Rika."

RUPERT

sees his Daddy is surprised

"Sir Jasper will make a great fuss."
Says Rupert. "He'll be cross with us..."

"Oh, no he won't," says Growler. "Why,
It was his fault that they got away."

But Daddy Bear is shocked to see
Constable Growler look scruffy!

"Young Rupert has some tale to tell!"
Laughs Growler, bidding them farewell.

"Won't Sir Jasper make a great fuss about the reindeer escaping?" asks Rupert. "Let him try!" Growler says. "I'll tell him it was his fault I didn't catch them. He and Scrogg held onto that reindeer just when I needed it to give chase. That's stopping a policeman doing his duty. Very serious that is."

PC Growler takes Rupert home. Rupert's Daddy gasps when he sees the state of Growler's uniform. "I fell off a reindeer," Growler volunteers. "Rupert will tell you all about it, I feel sure." Rupert grins. "Thanks for your help today, young Rupert," says Growler with a chuckle. "Now, goodnight all."

THE END

Try to colour these two pictures as carefully as you can.

Follow Rupert

John Harrold

in the DAILY ✠ EXPRESS
and the SUNDAY ✠ EXPRESS

Answers to Puzzles

Dot-to-dot
Rupert and Rika

Spot the Difference

1. *Pilot's goggles*
2. *Rupert's teacup missing*
3. *Flask missing*
4. *Bottom left - leaves missing*
5. *Support missing on shelter*
6. *Top left - root missing*
7. *Pilot's teacup changes colour*
8. *Sun changes colour*
9. *Part of Pilot's scarf missing*
10. *Willie Mouse's tail missing*

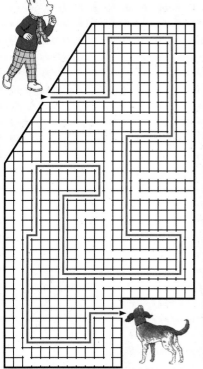

Find Charlie

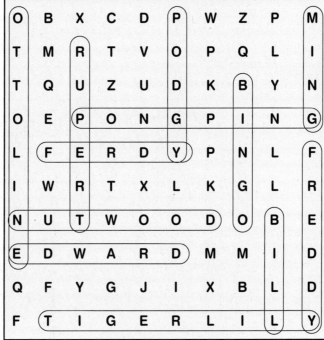

O	B	X	C	D	P	W	Z	P		M
T	M	R	T	V	O	P	Q	L		I
T	Q	U	Z	U	D	K	B	Y		N
O	E	P	O	N	G	P	I	N		G
L	F	E	R	D	Y	P	N	L		F
I	W	R	T	X	L	K	G	L		R
N	U	T	W	O	O	D	O	B		E
E	D	W	A	R	D	M	M	I		D
Q	F	Y	G	J	I	X	B	L		D
F	T	I	G	E	R	L	I	L		Y

Wordsearch

The publishers would like to thank the following for their invaluable help in compiling this book: Derek Unsworth; Michelle Stanistreet; Phil Toze; Rhona Crawford; Lucy and Daniel McGeever. A CIP catalogue record for this book is available from the British Library. All rights reserved. No part of this publication may be reproduced, stored in a retrieval system, or transmitted in any form or by any means, electronic, mechanical, photocopying, recording or otherwise, without the prior written permission of the copyright owner. Designed: James Bird. Colour reproduction by Scriveners, UK. Printed in Italy.